Mud Is Cake

Pam Muñoz Ryan

ILLUSTRATED BY

David McPhail

HYPERION BOOKS FOR CHILDREN
NEW YORK

FIRST EDITION
1 3 5 7 9 10 8 6 4 2

The artist used a bamboo reed pen, brown ink, and watercolor to create the art for this book.

Printed in Hong Kong

Library of Congress Cataloging-in-Publication Data
Ryan, Pam Muñoz.
Mud is cake / Pam Muñoz Ryan; illustrated by David McPhail.—1st ed.
p.   cm.
Summary: A brother and sister find that when they use their imagination
mud can become cake and they themselves can become almost anything.
ISBN 0-7868-0501-3 (hc)
[1. Imagination—Fiction. 2. Play—Fiction. 3. Stories in rhyme.] I. McPhail, David M., ill.
PZ8.3.R955 Mu 2002
E—dc21
2001039079

Visit www.hyperionchildrensbooks.com

To Annie Ryan: tiger *and* kitten
—P.M.R.

For Lachlan
—D.M.

Mud is cake
if you pretend
and don't really take a bite.

And juice is tea
with a fairy queen
if you act it out just right.

Porch is stage
when you imagine
thunderous applause.

Stick is wand
when you suppose
the magic it can cause.

Bear is friend
if you believe
that bears can see and hear.

And box is hideout
when you need
a secret atmosphere.

Pot is drum
when you invent
a noisy marching band.

Hole is tunnel
when you think
you'll reach another land.

Snow is fort
when you create
the place that you will play.

And tree is spaceship
if you trust
that it can fly away.

Tub is boat
if you sing out
that you've set sail again.

Book is door
if you escape
to where you've
never been.

Can is phone
when someone hopes
to hear the latest news.

And couch is store
when you display
a variety of shoes.

You are tiger,
strong and fierce,
a prowling, growling cat.

You are kitten,
soft and gentle,
curled on
someone's lap.

You are hero.
You are champion.
Declare you'll save the day!

Or if you choose,
you can be
the one who runs away.

You can be most anything
in dreams, or wide-awake.
If you agree that juice is tea . . .

. . . if you believe
that mud is cake.